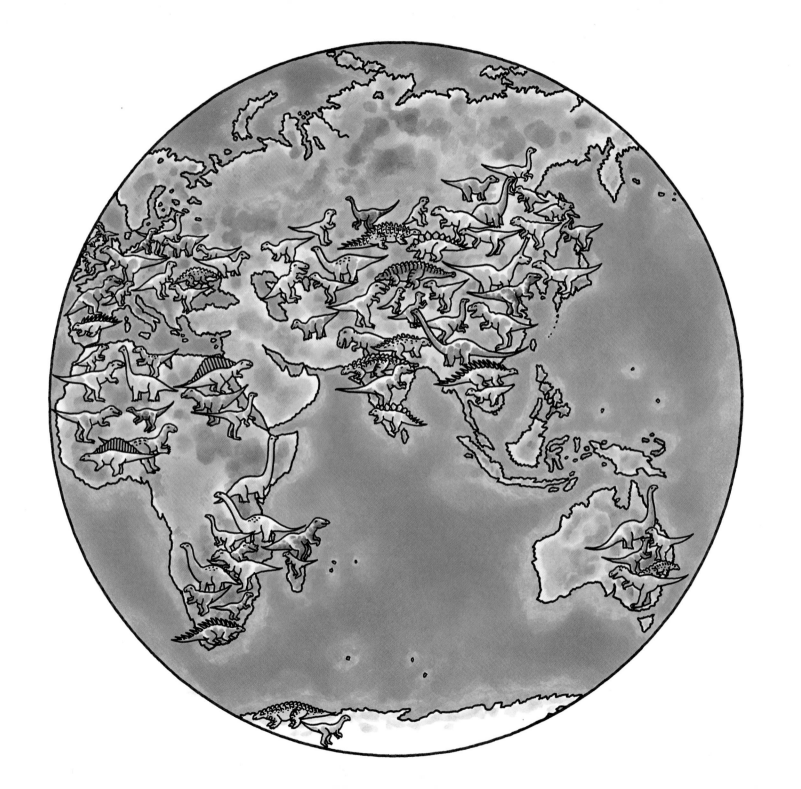

Bernard Most

Where to Look for a Dinosaur

Harcourt Brace Jovanovich, Publishers
San Diego   New York   London
Printed in Singapore

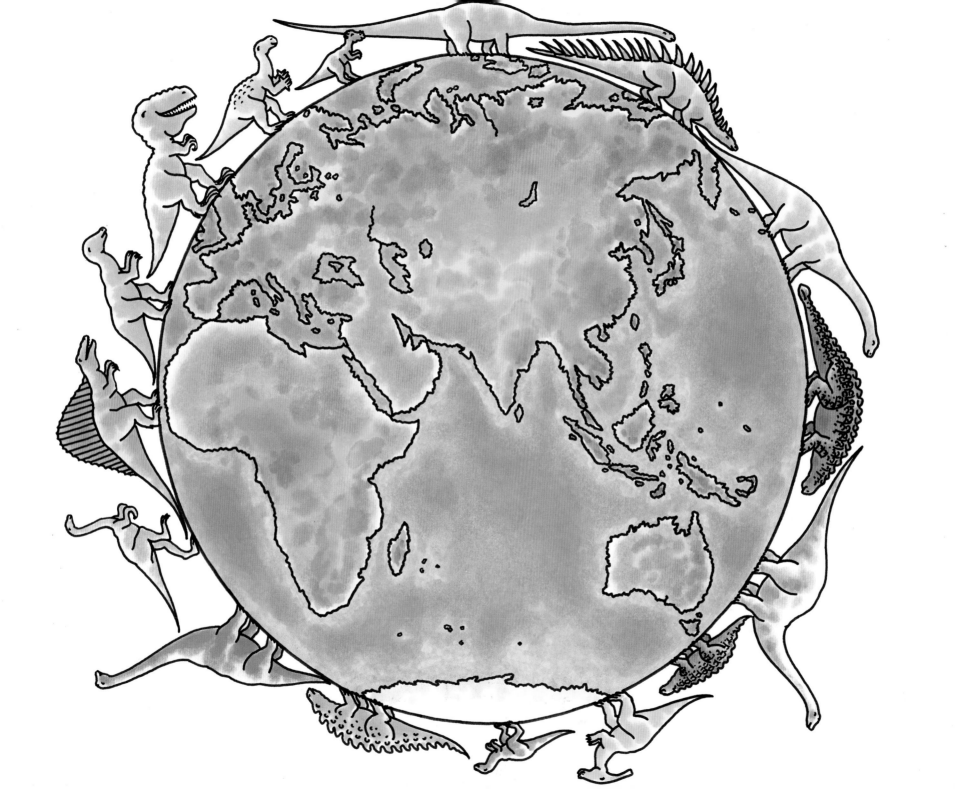

Library of Congress Cataloging-in-Publication Data
Most, Bernard.
Where to look for a dinosaur/by Bernard Most. — 1st ed.
p.   cm.
Summary: Describes various types of dinosaurs and where fossils have been found throughout the world. Features a list of museums with dinosaur collections.
ISBN 0-15-295616-6
1. Dinosaurs — Juvenile literature.   2. Dinosaurs — Catalogs and collections — Juvenile literature.   [1. Dinosaurs.]   I. Title.
CE862.D5M696   1993
567.9′1 — dc20   92-19443

First edition
A B C D E

Printed in Singapore

The illustrations in this book were done in Pantone markers on Bainbridge board 172, hot-press finish.
The display type was set in Elan by Central Graphics,
    San Diego, California.
The text type was set in Frutiger #55 by Thompson Type,
    San Diego, California.
Color separations by Bright Arts, Ltd., Singapore
Printed and bound by Tien Wah Press, Singapore
Production supervision by Warren Wallerstein and Diana Novak
Designed by Lydia D'moch

The author would like to thank HBJ's very own Diane-osaurus, also known as Senior Editor Diane D'Andrade, for her many creative contributions to this book.

The author wishes to acknowledge the following books as
    sources for the factual information contained in the text:
A Field Guide to Dinosaurs by David Lambert
Dinosaur Data Book by David Lambert
The Illustrated Dinosaur Dictionary by Helen Roney Sattler

More books by Bernard Most:

Happy Holidaysaurus!
Pets in Trumpets and Other Word-Play Riddles
A Dinosaur Named after Me
The Cow That Went OINK
The Littlest Dinosaurs
Dinosaur Cousins?
Whatever Happened to the Dinosaurs?
If the Dinosaurs Came Back
My Very Own Octopus

To my mother,
for her never-ending encouragement

Dinosaurs lived from 230 million years ago to 65 million years ago.

Fossils of dinosaurs have been found all around the world, and every day scientists are searching for new dinosaur fossils.

Wouldn't you like to look for a dinosaur? The best places to look are places where some have already been found. . . .

You can look for Arctosaurus (ark-ta-SAW-russ) in the Arctic.
This dinosaur's name means "Arctic lizard" because its fossils were found on an island north of the Arctic Circle.
Arctosaurus might be surprised by the "overgrown teeth" of today's Arctic walrus. Even Tyrannosaurus Rex didn't have teeth that big!

You can look for Albertosaurus (al-BERT-a-saw-russ) in Canada.

In Alberta's Dinosaur Provincial Park, dinosaur bones are preserved right where they were found among the unusual sandstone formations.

The Royal Canadian Mounted Police are good at tailing criminals. I wonder if they would be good at tailing dinosaurs?

You can look for Anchisaurus (ANG-kee-saw-russ) in Connecticut.
Because its fossils were found near Yale University, this dinosaur is also called Yaleosaurus (YALE-ee-a-saw-russ).
This plant eater liked to chew on soft plants, so I think it would have loved a taste of Ivy League life!

You can look for Silvisaurus (SIL-va-saw-russ) in Kansas.
This little armored dinosaur's name means "forest lizard" because
it was found in a Kansas forest. That's just the right place to look
for a plant eater.
I bet Silvisaurus would have loved the corn that grows in Kansas now!

You can look for Triceratops (try-SER-a-tops) in Montana.

Scientists think this three-horned dinosaur once roamed in great herds along vast ranges of North America.

It makes me want to sing, "Oh give me a home where the buffalo roam and the deer and the Triceratops play. . . ."

You can look for Acrocanthosaurus (ak-row-KANTH-a-saw-russ) in Oklahoma.
Found under layers and layers of rock, oil comes from the decay of
plants and animals that lived millions of years ago. That's why oil is called a
"fossil fuel."
Some oil pumps even remind me of dinosaurs!

You can look for Ammosaurus (AM-a-saw-russ) in Arizona.

The Grand Canyon is in Arizona, and geologists think some rocks there now may be over two billion years old, much older than dinosaurs.

I wonder if this dinosaur visited the Grand Canyon, and I wonder if the views were as beautiful then as they are now.

You can look for Alamosaurus (AL-a-mo-saw-russ) in Texas.

This large plant eater's name means "Alamo lizard." It was one of the last sauropods to live in North America.

From now on, whenever I hear the words "Remember the Alamo," I'm also going to remember the Alamosaurus!

You can look for Labocania (lab-o-KAY-nee-a) in Mexico.
This flesh-eating dinosaur with plenty of teeth was a lot like
Tyrannosaurus Rex but a little smaller.
Some of the stone carvings found among Mexican ruins make
me wonder if the ancient Mayans knew about dinosaurs.

You can look for Staurikosaurus (stor-IK-a-saw-russ) in Brazil.
I bet this dinosaur would have felt at home in a modern rain forest.
But because our rain forests are fast disappearing, many forms of
plant and animal life are in danger of disappearing, too — just as
Staurikosaurus did.

You can look for Saltasaurus (salt-a-SAW-russ) in Argentina.

This armor-backed dinosaur was able to rear up on its hind legs to feed on the tallest trees.

Gauchos or "South American cowboys" are expert horseback riders. Do you think Saltasaurus could throw a gaucho?

You can look for Titanosaurus (tie-TAN-a-saw-russ) in Uruguay.

Over 300 years of cattle raising has turned this South American country into a land of prairies. Many plants and animals have disappeared.

Too bad this "titanic" plant eater can't come back to warn us about endangering plant and animal life.

You can look for Lesothosaurus (less-OTH-a-saw-russ) in Lesotho.
This beautiful mountainous country in Africa is known as "a hiker's paradise."
I think this energetic little dinosaur, with its very long legs, would be an excellent hiker.

You can look for Barosaurus (BAR-a-saw-russ) in Zimbabwe.

This dinosaur once lived in the same place we find one of the world's largest waterfalls, Victoria Falls.

I wonder how long ago this beautiful waterfall was formed. Do you think the dinosaurs ever saw a rainbow over Victoria Falls?

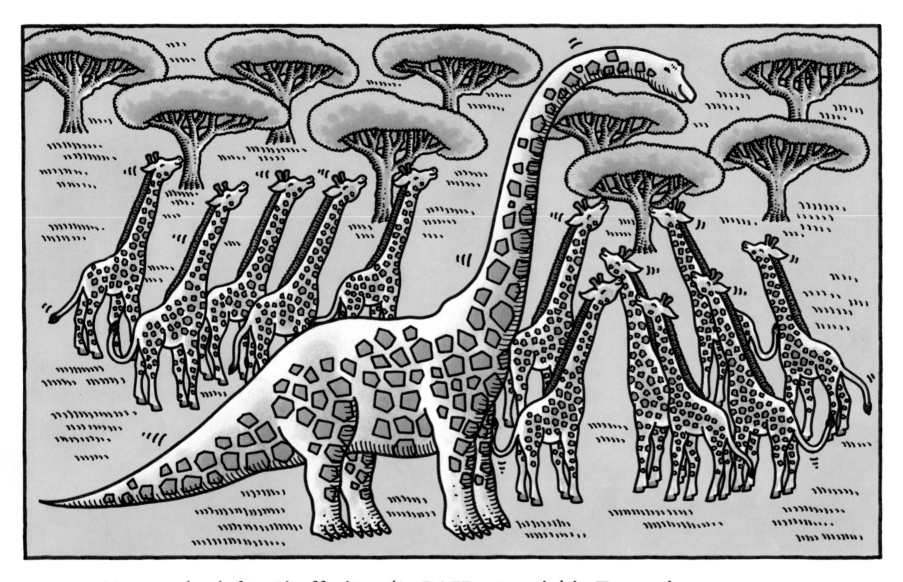

You can look for Giraffatitan (Ja-RAFF-a-tye-tin) in Tanzania.
It's fitting that one of the tallest dinosaurs, named "gigantic giraffe," was found in the country with the tallest peak in Africa, Mt. Kilimanjaro!
I would love to see the look on the faces of Tanzania's giraffes if they ever had the chance to meet Giraffatitan.

You can look for Spinosaurus (SPY-na-saw-russ) in Egypt.
Some scientists think the giant sail-like fin on its back was for defense. Others say this fin controlled body temperature.
I wonder which riddle we will solve first, the riddle of the Sphinx or the riddle of the Spinosaurus.

You can look for more kinds of dinosaurs in China than anyplace else.
So many dinosaurs have been discovered in China, I bet they could
fill the Great Wall of China, which is over 1,500 miles long.
You can look for Shantungosaurus (shan-TUNG-a-saw-russ).
You can look for Mamenchisaurus (ma-MEN-chee-saw-russ).

You can look for Szechuanosaurus (set-CHEW-ON-a-saw-russ).
You can look for Tsintaosaurus (chin-TAY-o-saw-russ).
You can look for Chingkankosaurus (ching-KANG-kow-saw-russ).
You can look for Yangchuanosaurus (yang-CHEW-ON-a-saw-russ).
You can look for . . .

You can look for Kagasaurus (ka-ga-SAW-russ) in Japan.
Scientists have found fossils of its very big, sharp teeth. They think this dinosaur was a large two-legged meat eater.
When you look at dragons in the art of Japan, China, and Korea, don't they remind you of dinosaurs?

You can look for Indosaurus (in-doe-SAW-russ) in India.
It was a member of the family called "tigers of the Dinosaur Age."
Tigers, once very common all over Asia, are now an endangered species. But India is creating many reserves to protect the tiger from extinction. I think Indosaurus would be pleased.

You can look for Itemirus (eye-TIM-ih-russ) in Russia.

Scientists think this small two-legged dinosaur had a very well developed sense of balance.

Russia is famous for the Moscow Ballet and the Bolshoi Ballet. Wouldn't it be fun to see a performance with graceful Itemirus?

You can look for Rhabdodon (RAB-da-don) in Austria.

This speedy plant eater with very long legs was a member of the dinosaur family nicknamed "dinosaur gazelles."

I'm sure this dinosaur could do well at one of the international skiing competitions at Innsbruck, Austria.

You can look for Saltopus (SALT-o-pus) in Scotland.

This little two-legged dinosaur may have been the earliest European dinosaur. Some think it was one of the smartest dinosaurs and made good use of its five fingers.

I think it could have learned to play the bagpipes.

You can look for Austrosaurus (OSS-tra-saw-russ) in Australia.
This giant plant eater's fossils were found in the "land down under" where the koala makes its home.
Don't you think koala families would have a great time climbing up and down this dinosaur's very long neck?

You can look for Iguanodon (ig-WAN-a-don) all over the world.
Fossils of this peaceful plant eater have been found on every continent, and it was among the first dinosaurs to be discovered.
Because it has been found in more places on Earth than any other dinosaur, I think it should be the official dinosaur of the United Nations.

You can look in these museums for some of the dinosaurs that have already been found:

Canada

Drumheller, Alberta
Tyrrell Museum of Palaeontology

Edmonton, Alberta
Provincial Museum of Alberta

Ottawa, Ontario
National Museum of Natural Sciences

Toronto, Ontario
Royal Ontario Museum

United States

Amherst, Massachusetts
Pratt Museum

Ann Arbor, Michigan
University of Michigan Exhibit Museum

Austin, Texas
Texas Memorial Museum

Berkeley, California
University of California Museum of Paleontology

Boulder, Colorado
University Natural History Museum

Bozeman, Montana
Museum of the Rockies

Buffalo, New York
Buffalo Museum of Science

Cambridge, Massachusetts
Museum of Comparative Zoology, Harvard University

Chicago, Illinois
Field Museum of Natural History

Cleveland, Ohio
Natural History Museum

Denver, Colorado
Denver Museum of Natural History

East Lansing, Michigan
The Museum, Michigan State University

Flagstaff, Arizona
Museum of Northern Arizona

Jensen, Utah
Dinosaur National Monument

Laramie, Wyoming
The Geological Museum

Lincoln, Nebraska
University of Nebraska State Museum

Los Angeles, California
L. A. County Museum of Natural History

New Haven, Connecticut
Peabody Museum of Natural History, Yale University

New York, New York
American Museum of Natural History

Norman, Oklahoma
Stovall Museum, University of Oklahoma

Philadelphia, Pennsylvania
Academy of Natural Sciences

Pittsburgh, Pennsylvania
Carnegie Museum of Natural History

Princeton, New Jersey
Museum of Natural History, Princeton University

Provo, Utah
Earth Science Museum, Brigham Young University

St. Paul, Minnesota
The Science Museum of Minnesota

Salt Lake City, Utah
Utah Museum of Natural History, University of Utah

Washington, D.C.
National Museum of Natural History, Smithsonian Institution

Mexico
Mexico City
Natural History Museum

Brazil
Rio de Janeiro
National Museum

Argentina
Buenos Aires
Argentine Museum of Natural Sciences

Zimbabwe
Harare
National Museum of Zimbabwe

Niger
Niamey
National Museum of Niger

Morocco
Rabat
Museum of Earth Sciences

South Africa
Cape Town
South African Museum

Johannesburg
Bernard Price Institute of Palaeontology

China
Beijing
Beijing Natural History Museum
Museum of the Institute of Vertebrate Paleontology and Paleoanthropology

Beipei, Sichuan
Beipei Museum

Chengdu, Sichuan
Museum of Chengdu College of Geology

Hohhot, Inner Mongolia
Inner Mongolia Museum

Shanghai
Shanghai Museum

Tianjin
Tianjin Museum of Natural History

Zigong, Sichuan
Zigong Dinosaur Museum

Taiwan
Taichung
National Museum of Natural Science

Mongolia
Ulan Bator
Academy of Sciences

Japan
Kitakyūshū, Fukuoka
Kitakyūshū Museum of Natural History

Kyōto, Honshū
Kyōto Municipal Science Center for Youth

Ōsaka, Honshū
Ōsaka Museum of Natural History

Tokyo, Honshū
National Science Museum

Toyohashi, Aichi
Toyohashi Museum of Natural History

India
Calcutta
Geology Museum, Indian Statistical Institute

Russia
Moscow
Paleontological Institute

Austria
Vienna
Natural History Museum

Scotland
Edinburgh
Royal Museum of Scotland

England
London
The Natural History Museum

Poland
Warsaw
Paleobiology Institute

Spain
Madrid
Natural Science Museum

Italy
Venice
Civic Museum of Natural History

France
Paris
National Museum of Natural History

Germany
Berlin
Natural History Museum, Humboldt University

Frankfurt am Main
Senckenberg Nature Museum

Stuttgart
State Museum for Natural History

Sweden
Uppsala
Paleontological Museum, Uppsala University

Switzerland
Geneva
Natural History Museum

Australia
Sydney, New South Wales
Australian Museum

Fortitude Valley, Queensland
Queensland Museum

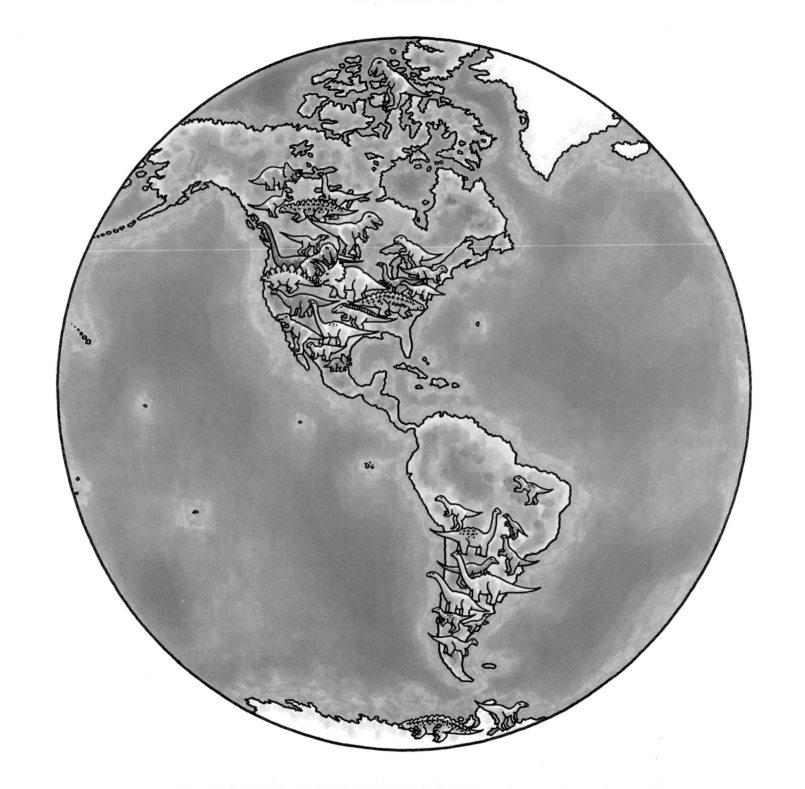